Hunky Heartbreaker

Also from Kendall Ryan

For a complete list of Kendall's books, visit:
www.kendallryanbooks.com/all-books/

Hunky Heartbreaker

A Whiskey Kisses Novella

By Kendall Ryan

1001 Dark Nights

EVIL EYE

CONCEPTS

Hunky Heartbreaker
A Whiskey Kisses Novella
By Kendall Ryan

1001 Dark Nights

Copyright 2018 Kendall Ryan
ISBN: 978-1-948050-37-1

Foreword: Copyright 2014 M. J. Rose

Published by Evil Eye Concepts, Incorporated

Acknowledgments from the Author

A huge thank you to my entire dream team. I'm especially grateful to MJ Rose and Liz Berry. You are both such professionals and so lovely in everything you do. I'm in awe of all you have accomplished.

A huge bear hug to all of the book bloggers and readers for your excitement about Duke and Valentina's story. I am so appreciative of each and every review you left.

I'm blessed to have so many amazing people in my life rooting me on, especially my sweet husband. Finally, I'm so incredibly blessed to have YOU as a reader. Thank you!

Sign up for the 1001 Dark Nights Newsletter
and be entered to win a Tiffany Key necklace.

There's a contest every month!

Go to www.1001DarkNights.com for more information.

As a bonus, all subscribers will receive a free copy of
Discovery Bundle Three
Featuring stories by
Sidney Bristol, Darcy Burke, T. Gephart
Stacey Kennedy, Adriana Locke
JB Salsbury, and Erika Wilde

One Thousand and One Dark Nights

Once upon a time, in the future...

*I was a student fascinated with stories and learning.
I studied philosophy, poetry, history, the occult, and
the art and science of love and magic. I had a vast
library at my father's home and collected thousands
of volumes of fantastic tales.*

*I learned all about ancient races and bygone
times. About myths and legends and dreams of all
people through the millennium. And the more I read
the stronger my imagination grew until I discovered
that I was able to travel into the stories... to actually
become part of them.*

*I wish I could say that I listened to my teacher
and respected my gift, as I ought to have. If I had, I
would not be telling you this tale now.
But I was foolhardy and confused, showing off
with bravery.*

*One afternoon, curious about the myth of the
Arabian Nights, I traveled back to ancient Persia to
see for myself if it was true that every day Shahryar
(Persian: شهريار, "king") married a new virgin, and then
sent yesterday's wife to be beheaded. It was written
and I had read, that by the time he met Scheherazade,
the vizier's daughter, he'd killed one thousand
women.*

*Something went wrong with my efforts. I arrived
in the midst of the story and somehow exchanged
places with Scheherazade — a phenomena that had
never occurred before and that still to this day, I
cannot explain.*

*Now I am trapped in that ancient past. I have
taken on Scheherazade's life and the only way I can
protect myself and stay alive is to do what she did to
protect herself and stay alive.*

*Every night the King calls for me and listens as I spin tales.
And when the evening ends and dawn breaks, I stop at a
point that leaves him breathless and yearning for more.
And so the King spares my life for one more day, so that
he might hear the rest of my dark tale.*

*As soon as I finish a story... I begin a new
one... like the one that you, dear reader, have before
you now.*

Chapter One

Duke

"I'd like to thank each and every one of you for joining us this evening," my twin brother Luke said, smiling as he looked out on the crowd gathered in our bar.

"Ten years ago, my brother and I decided to take this distillery and turn it into something we could be proud of. It's been a long and difficult road, but tonight, I'm proud to announce not only that our whiskey will now be sold in stores all across Texas, but also that our brand-spanking-new tasting rooms are open for business."

The crowd cheered, and Luke turned to me with a look on his face like I needed to say something too. I stared back at him for a split second, my mind a hair fuzzier than I wanted it to be in that moment. That's what I got for pre-gaming the grand opening of my own distillery, I supposed.

But I'd be damned if I was about to let Luke steal my reputation as the fun-loving, charming-as-hell Wilder brother.

"Here's to turning this run-down, piece of shit piss-stillery into an honest-to-goodness, respectable establishment. To Wilder Whiskey!"

"To Wilder Whiskey!" the crowd roared back.

We drank, the familiar burn hitting the back of my throat before spreading warmth throughout my entire body. Luke and I rolled the heavy wood and iron barn door open, ushering our guests into the brand-new tasting room for the very first time.

If our old tasting room was pretty good, our new one was fucking badass. Luke's wife, Charlotte, had given us some big-city decorating tips, and for as much as I liked to tease her for having a stick up her ass, she had good taste. We'd swapped out the brown velvet armchairs and rustic table for a wraparound oak bar with iron stools and four custom-made tables for extra seating. We kept the wall opposite the bar full of windows, which at that moment perfectly framed the blood-orange sun setting in the wide-open Texas sky.

Luke clapped a hand on my shoulder as we stood in the doorway watching the crowd fill the room.

"Proud of us, brother. We really pulled it off."

"Turns out Dad didn't totally fuck us over after all."

Luke grimaced at the mention of our alcoholic father, who ran this place into the ground before passing away and leaving it to us. I threw my arm around his shoulders and shook him.

"Hey, I'm not trying to bring the mood down. But just look at this place. We did this. And we did good, no matter what little he left us with."

"Yeah, I guess you're right."

"Hell yeah, I'm right! Now come on, it's time to drink and

be merry and do whatever else you do when you make a decade-long dream come true."

We parted ways, Luke joining Charlotte at a table by the windows, leaving me to my own devices. Across the room, I spotted two beautiful, familiar faces, and suddenly I knew exactly how I wanted to spend my evening.

Walking over to the bar, I ordered two of our signature cocktails and had them sent over to the women. Within ten minutes, my plan had been perfectly executed, and they'd both joined me at my corner of the bar, each sitting on one of my knees, giggling and fawning over my every word.

"Well, who'd have ever thought that the three of us would reunite one day? And in my very own distillery? How long has it been since this threesome spent one of our wild nights together?" I drawled, my hands wandering over their backs.

The two women exchanged a knowing look, the one on my right tossing her strawberry blond locks over her shoulder.

"I'd say it's been at least three years. What do you think, Kelly?"

"I don't know, Kaylie, I think it's more like four or five," the brunette responded, trailing a red-tipped fingernail along my jaw.

"Well, I remember it like it was yesterday."

Kelly and Kaylie giggled, each of them leaning in closer to put their impossibly pushed-up breasts on full display. I'd known them both since high school, their reputations for flirting and playing the field rivaling my own. But it wasn't until they both came home for winter break in college that the three of us got together for one of the more memorable flings of my career.

"Rumor has it you moved out of the Wilder compound after Luke got married," Kelly said, dragging her fingertips along my bicep.

"We'd love to see your new place sometime soon," Kaylie added, her free hand settling on my upper thigh.

Before I could respond, Luke appeared out of nowhere, the look on his face grim.

"Hate to break this party up, ladies, but I'm afraid I need to talk to my brother alone."

"Awww," Kaylie whined, pushing her lower lip out in a fake pout.

"If you beauties will excuse me, it seems there's some unwanted business I have to attend to," I said, kissing them both on the cheek before following Luke into the back room.

"All right, man, what could possibly be so pressing that we had to leave our own party?"

Luke narrowed his eyes and crossed his arms.

"We've got a problem. Apparently our logo is too similar to a trademarked image."

I bristled. I'd drawn and designed our logo from scratch months ago. It wasn't anything too fancy, but still, I'd put a full month's worth of work into it, and I was damn proud of it.

"Okay, so if we have to change it, we will. Not like we'll need to pay extra for a designer."

"It's not that simple. They want damages in excess of eight million dollars. We just got this place off the ground. We don't have that kind of money."

I took a step back, feeling like the wind just got knocked out of me. Eight million bucks? Who the fuck did these people think they were?

The door to the room opened, briefly letting the roar of the party in before it closed again, muffling the sounds of the voices and music. Charlotte appeared around the corner, her brows knitted together in concern.

"There you guys are, I've been looking all over for you two. Everything okay back here?"

"Far from it," I growled, pushing my hands roughly through my hair. Fucking figures that the moment I felt like I finally had our business under control, some asshole had to come along to try to take it all away.

Luke filled Charlotte in on the situation while I paced around the room, desperately trying to come up with a solution.

"My friend Valentina is a lawyer," Charlotte said, slipping her arm around Luke's waist.

"Who?"

"Valentina, my best friend who lives in LA? You met her at our wedding."

"Whoopdie-fucking-do, she can't do shit for us all the way in California." I could feel myself becoming defensive. I'd gotten completely trashed at their wedding, so honestly, my memory was a little foggy.

Luke shot me a dirty look. I knew I was being an asshole, but I couldn't help it. Not when everything I'd worked so hard for was on the line.

"That might be true, but lucky for you two, she'll be here tomorrow. I'll call and set up a meeting with her in the morning, so you can consult with her then," Charlotte said with just a tinge of coldness in her voice. She'd learned to expect a few rough edges from me since becoming a part of my family, but I already knew Luke would chew me out for being a hot-head later. Damn, sometimes it sucks being the younger brother. Even if only by a few minutes.

"Fine, let's see if your hotshot lawyer friend can help us out. Thank you," I added, forcing a smile at them both.

Luke put his arm around Charlotte and the two of them rejoined the party, leaving me to stew in my own frustration.

I knew my brother was in love and seeing him happier than he'd been in years really did make me happy. But I couldn't help being a little salty at how little he seemed to care about this. Just a couple years ago, this distillery was all we had besides each other. But now Luke had Charlotte, and this place was really all I had left to show for myself. It was the love of my life, practically my baby, and you'd better believe I was protective as hell of it.

Those two babes in my lap earlier? They didn't do a damn thing for me. Because even before Luke had Charlotte, I was always the twin who had something to prove. Growing up, Luke was better at everything. He made varsity football our freshman year, got straight As all throughout school, and quickly developed a reputation as the better, more stable, more successful Wilder twin. I had a hard time in school because of my dyslexia, and it felt like I always had to work ten times harder to make sure I didn't become the dumb twin—or worse, the town idiot. But ever since Luke settled down, it seemed like I was getting closer and closer to becoming the town drunk, and that was even worse.

I knew I had to do everything in my power to save the distillery. And if that meant shutting up and taking orders from a hotshot LA lawyer was the only way to do that, so be it.

Besides, if memory served me right, she wasn't so bad to look at, either.

Chapter Two

Duke

I woke up to a pounding headache and a tongue drier than the Sahara Desert. I grabbed my phone from the bedside table, checking the time through squinted eyes. 9:27. There were a couple missed calls from Kelly. She was probably just mad I didn't take her and Kaylie home with me. Not that I was ever really planning on it. If there's one thing I learned from the last time the three of us spent the night, it's that mornings after are even worse with an extra person in the mix.

After splashing some water on my face and throwing my sweat-soaked shirt in the hamper, I made my way to the kitchen. Coffee, then shower. That was the plan. Even if walking down those damn stairs made my head throb harder with every step.

When I reached the kitchen, I stopped dead in my tracks. Now, I'd never had a hangover so bad that I hallucinated, but in that moment, I was about ready to believe it could happen. Because standing in the middle of my kitchen was a smoking hot woman in a tight black skirt and a red silk blouse, with her arms crossed and back to me.

Not that I was complaining about the view.

Maybe I didn't remember the end of last night as well as I thought I did. I could have sworn I came home alone, but according to the vision in red just a few yards away, there was a lot of late night action I was forgetting. But even if my brain was still a little hazy from the booze, judging by the stirring in my boxer briefs, my dick remembered just fine.

"Good morning, darlin'. Could I interest you in some breakfast sausage?"

The woman turned, her long, dark curls swinging around her shoulders. A look of disgust quickly washed over her face as her eyes locked on my bulge.

"*Ay dios mio*, you've got to be fucking kidding me," she muttered, immediately taking her briefcase from the counter and marching to the front door, her red-bottomed heels clacking loudly on the hardwood.

"What's the matter?" I asked, stumbling after her.

"Last time I do a favor for a friend," she said under her breath, slamming the front door shut behind her.

Favor. Friend. Beautiful woman in a pencil skirt. Charlotte's hotshot lawyer friend from Los Angeles.

Oh fuck.

"Hey, uh, Valencia, wait up!"

I burst through the door to find her paused on the top step of the porch. She turned sharply to look me dead on, the fire in her eyes enough to burn me straight through.

"It's Valentina," she spat, crossing her arms and cocking her hip to the side.

"Valentina, right. My mistake. Listen, I'm really sorry

about all this. We were out late last night for—"

"For the opening, I know. I was supposed to be there, but something came up at work. So instead, I got my ass onto a last-minute redeye to make it in time for our meeting this morning, but clearly you had other things in mind," she said, her eyes flitting to my quickly-softening cock before turning again to leave.

"No, please, don't go. This is completely unprofessional, I know—"

"That's the understatement of the century."

"But I promise, if you give me a chance, we can turn this meeting around."

"Is it still a meeting when one person shows up with his dick out?"

"Oh, trust me, sweetheart, if my dick was out, you'd know it."

"Sure, as long as I brought a magnifying glass with me."

I paused, standing up a little straighter. She squared her shoulders, and our eyes locked, the tension between us thick enough to cut with a knife.

If we were going to make this work, I knew I had to be the one to budge. But dammit if this woman didn't make me want to blow my lid.

"Look, I'm sorry. Please stay. If not for me, then for Luke and Charlotte."

Valentina sighed and put a hand on her hip.

"Fine. Put some goddamn pants on first, and then we'll talk."

Within fifteen minutes, Valentina and I were walking into the local coffee shop. After throwing on a pair of dark jeans and a gray T-shirt, I convinced her that moving to a second location was probably a good idea. I drove us over to Sue's Brews, the best—and only—place for coffee in town.

I led us to my usual corner booth, simply smiling and waving at the hostess as we seated ourselves. Sue's was really more of a café than a coffee shop, with lots of tables and waitresses and such, and I could tell by the look on her face when we walked in that Valentina was expecting something different. I felt a smirk pull the corner of my lip up as I imagined her surprise at how different this place was from the hoity-toity places she probably got her coffee in Los Angeles.

"Not your cup of tea?" I asked after we sat down, nodding my head at the baby blue vinyl bar stools.

Valentina shook her head, propping her elbows up on the table.

"It's just that when you said coffee shop, I assumed it would be…something a little more…" She left the rest of her sentence unfinished, but I was assuming she meant something from this century.

"Well, Sue's is the only place in town. And we've got a lot of coffee drinkers here in Shady Grove."

"Yeah, I can see that," she said, shifting uncomfortably in her seat. The place was pretty busy—it was a Sunday morning, after all—and as usual, the locals weren't doing a great job of not staring at the out-of-towner.

"Don't worry about them, just sniffing out the new meat. Speaking of, have you eaten yet?"

"I haven't, actually. Took that redeye from LA, remember?"

"Lucky for you, Sue's has the best breakfast in town. But

don't tell anyone I said that."

Valentina nodded, stretching her full lips into a straight line and miming like she was locking them up.

"Well, I'll be damned. Duke Wilder, based on how you were drinking last night, I would have put money on it that you would have been dead to the world until at least next Tuesday."

Our waitress appeared next to the table and gave me a playful punch on the arm.

"Oh, come on, Jenny, you know me better than that. No amount of drinking could keep me from seeing that face of yours the next morning."

Jenny giggled, and Valentina rolled her eyes, muttering something in Spanish under her breath.

"What can I get you two today?" Jenny asked, smiling broadly at us both.

"Just the usual for me, Jen," I replied, handing her my menu.

Valentina clicked her tongue as she scanned the small list of breakfast foods and drinks.

"If you don't see what you're looking for, just let me know. We'll make just about anything for a friend of the Wilders." Jenny leaned an elbow on the back of Valentina's side of the booth.

"Oh, that won't be necessary," Valentina said without looking up, clearly struggling to find something she wanted on the menu. I'd watched Charlotte try to order food in Shady Grove enough times to know that she'd have a hard time finding the low-calorie, low-carb, fat-free, practically cardboard option she was looking for.

"Are you sure? You look like a woman who knows what she wants," I said, cocking my head to the side.

Valentina arched a perfectly sculpted eyebrow at me before turning to Jenny.

"I'll have an egg white omelet with spinach and tomato, and a non-fat latte with a dash of cinnamon, please."

"I think we can do that. I'll go put your orders in, and then I'll be right back with your coffees."

As soon as Jenny walked away, Valentina pulled a folder out of her bag, opening it to show me some forms she'd filled out.

"So, Luke and Charlotte explained your situation to me over the phone last night, and I think I figured out your best option moving forward. I've put together a countersuit."

She slid a form in front of me, but I didn't look it at. Didn't even touch it.

"I don't want to countersue. I just want them to drop the lawsuit."

Valentina shook her head. "They're not going to do that. I did some digging on these guys, and they are nasty. The only way we'll get them to drop it in a reasonable amount of time is if we countersue for a lot more money."

I sighed, leaning back into the blue vinyl and running my hands through my hair. Figures that the one time I think I made something good, something I could be proud of, a couple of fucking assholes with a trademark decide to make my life hell.

What those assholes didn't realize? I had one badass lawyer on my side.

And she was sexy as hell when she talked business.

"All right, I'm in," I said, extending my hand across the table. Valentina smirked at the gesture but shook on it anyway, her tanned skin warm against my palm.

Jenny returned with our food, and the sight of my full country breakfast next to Valentina's egg white omelet was laughable. Her eyes grew wide as she took in my meal: two eggs sunny side up, two thick cut slices of bacon, breakfast potatoes, and a side of biscuits and gravy.

"That's your usual?" she asked, taking a small bite of her meal.

"Takes a lot to look this good."

I puffed my chest and flexed a bicep at her, but she just rolled her eyes.

"Charlotte warned me about you and your ways."

"My *ways*?"

Valentina set her fork down, folding her hands and resting them on the table.

"This engagement will be strictly by the books. All that strutting and swagger might get you laid every once in a while, but that's not about to happen here. I've got a job to do, and that's all."

I raised my hands in surrender, shrugging and shaking my head. "Fine by me. You're the boss."

"Good. Glad that's settled."

I nodded, and we continued eating, but in the back of my mind I knew it was all a lie. She could tell herself all she wanted that there was nothing between us, that she wasn't picking up what I was putting down. But if there's one thing I know, it's women, and this one was definitely into me.

I gave it three days, tops, before I got in her panties. We

were both grown-ups. We could keep it professional.

But there was no way in hell I was letting her fly back to LA that next week without a taste.

Chapter Three

Valentina

What the hell do you wear to Sunday dinner in the freaking middle of nowhere?

Pulling a third printed top over my head, I let out a loud, exasperated sigh as I tossed it into a pile with the rest of the rejects. I went back to rifling through my suitcase, pushing various fabrics and colors aside in search of an outfit that would make me feel cool, calm, and collected—basically the exact opposite of how I was currently feeling.

It's not like I'd never been to Shady Grove before. When I'd flown out for Luke and Charlotte's wedding, I'd thought the town was cute enough, and on some level, I understood why Charlotte had decided to stay. But something about this place just didn't sit right with me. Maybe it had to do with the lack of Starbucks or anything remotely familiar, but I wasn't the kind of girl to have a panic attack over a lack of creature comforts. No, my problem with that place wasn't a what. It was a who.

An arrogant, frustrating, sexy-as-hell who.

Duke Wilder.

My fingers landed on a soft, silky piece of fabric, and I immediately pulled it out of the rat's nest. I held it out, the beautiful marigold dress unfurling before me. Charlotte had convinced me to buy it when we were out shopping the year before, but I'd never worn it. Honestly, I'd only thrown it in my suitcase to make her happy. But with only a few minutes before I was officially late to my own welcome dinner, it was the only option I had left.

After slipping the dress on, I swept my hair to the side, wrestling my dark, unruly curls into a loose braid over my shoulder. Pulling out a few pieces in the front to frame my face, I took a step back to check my reflection in the floor-length mirror. The dress hung just right around my body: it cinched at the waist, its hemline just brushing the midpoint of my calf, the off-the-shoulder cut perfectly showcasing my tanned shoulders.

How is this the first time I'm wearing this dress? I really needed to stop doubting Charlotte's taste.

Slipping on a pair of strappy leather sandals, I slung my purse strap onto my shoulder and walked out the front door. If there was one thing I was grateful for that night, it was that the walk to Luke and Charlotte's was short. After waking up at an ungodly hour for the redeye and then gritting my teeth all through breakfast with the official pain in my ass Duke, I was pretty damn tired. Staying in the guest house just a short walk away from Charlotte's was one hell of a blessing.

When I got to their door, I rang the bell, taking a step back to look around and admire the porch. There were a couple of chairs, and the whole thing was so cute and country,

I half-expected to find a porch swing. It might not have been my cup of tea, but I couldn't deny that there was something charming about this whole small-town living thing.

The door swung open, and my stomach dropped when I saw the green-eyed, dimpled face smiling at me from the doorway.

Puta madre.

"Hey there, darlin', long time no see." Duke raised one arm over his head and rested his elbow against the doorjamb, leaning his muscular body in a way that made all kinds of dirty thoughts cross my mind.

"Nice to see you remembered to put clothes on this time," I said, trying my best to make my once-over of his body seem cold and disinterested, despite the familiar ache between my legs. Just looking at his hips brought me right back to our initial meeting in his kitchen that morning. Let's just say those boxer briefs left little to the imagination.

And what I saw? Was way bigger than I ever could have dreamt up.

"Only the best for you." He stepped aside and ushered me through the door, his fingertips just grazing the small of my back.

Goddammit if even the slightest touch of his didn't make me weak in the knees.

"I can't believe you're here!" Charlotte squealed, rounding the corner from the kitchen and practically knocking me over with a hug.

"Almost wasn't sure I'd make it," I replied, watching Duke leave us to say our hellos out of the corner of my eye.

"Tell me everything. Was the flight okay? How's the LA

apartment? Do you have everything you need in the guest house?"

Once Duke was out of earshot, I grabbed Charlotte's arm, pulling her into the nearest bathroom.

"You could have warned me he'd be here," I whispered, jerking my head in the direction Duke had left from.

"Who, Duke? I thought he would have said something during your meeting."

"Well, you thought wrong. I almost had a fucking heart attack when he answered the door."

"Why, is something wrong? Did the meeting go south this morning?"

"No, the meeting was fine. Well, sort of. I don't know, it was just...weird."

Charlotte took a step back, crossing her arms and giving me a knowing look.

"He made a pass at you, didn't he? Oh, god, I'm sorry, Val, I tried to warn you about him."

"No, it's not like that. I mean, sure, he was flirty, but I told him at the end of breakfast that nothing would happen between us, and he agreed to keep it professional."

Charlotte nodded, but she didn't look convinced.

"I'm serious, Char. Sure, he's attractive in a rugged kind of way, but none of that matters. I'm here to do a job, and that's it. Case closed."

"Whatever you say, Val. I support you, no matter what."

We looped arms and walked out of the bathroom. When we entered the kitchen, we found the two brothers standing by the table, sipping what I assumed was their own whiskey.

"Good to see you again, Valentina," Luke said, putting his

arm around me for a side hug.

"I just wish I was here for a less lawyer-y reason."

"Well, we appreciate your help. My brother filled me in on the meeting earlier, and we have full confidence in your legal guidance."

Duke dipped his chin in agreement, and my stomach flip-flopped at the thought of the two brothers talking about our meeting. What did Duke say about me? Did he think I was some fast-paced, know-it-all asshole who wouldn't make it three days in his town? Suddenly, I was determined to make it work here, creature comforts be damned.

"Glad to hear it."

"All right, enough business talk. Let's eat!" Charlotte said, motioning for us to take a seat. She'd decorated their long farmhouse table with wildflowers and fresh fruit, neatly arranged around large platters of food.

Charlotte and I sat on one side, and the men sat on the other. Seeing Luke and Duke right next to each other was a little unsettling, but even after only one day with Duke, I was starting to notice the subtle differences between them. And not just the small ways their hair fell differently, or the slight change in mole placement. The way they carried themselves was different, their speech patterns, how they held a drink. Not to mention how only one of them could make me feel like he saw right through me with just a look.

"Sure you're okay with that brisket, darlin'? There's a good amount of marble in it, you know," Duke said, raising his brows at me and motioning to the piece of meat on my plate.

Without breaking eye contact, I sliced myself a hefty bite

and placed it in my mouth. After chewing and swallowing, I turned to Charlotte.

"It's delicious."

"You'll have to thank Luke for that one. I'm just getting a handle on heart-healthier versions of his favorite sides."

I raised my glass to Luke, who simply clinked his against mine in response.

"You should have seen her at Sue's this morning. Egg white and veggie omelet. If I didn't know any better, I would have thought she was saving it for her pet rabbit later."

"If you want to die of a heart attack at forty-five, be my guest. I, on the other hand, plan on keeping my arteries clear for the foreseeable future. No offense," I added, nodding at Luke.

"None taken," he replied, giving Charlotte an amused look.

We kept on like that for the rest of dinner, the conversation light and easy until Duke or I felt the need to take a jab at one another. Part of me worried that I was being too openly rude to my hosts and clients, but a larger part of me couldn't resist. Sparring with Duke was fun—and easy. It was like we knew exactly which buttons to push to drive each other crazy.

After dinner, we all took our drinks to the front porch for a night cap. I was really feeling tired by that point, my exhaustion mixing with the whiskey to put a warm, comfortable haze over everything.

Charlotte sat on Luke's lap in one chair, and Duke leaned against the railing so I could sit in the other. Luke began explaining his idea for a new signature cocktail at the distillery, which was already blowing up with tours and guests in the tasting room. I could feel my eyelids growing heavy, the warm Texas breeze moving gently against my skin. After a few minutes, I woke with a start to Duke's fingertips brushing against my shoulder.

"Come on, sleeping beauty, I'll walk you home."

I didn't argue, instead thanking Luke and hugging Charlotte goodbye.

"Sorry I'm such a party pooper. You know if it was any other day, I'd be down to drink the night away on this porch."

"Don't worry about it, Val. You've had a long day. We have plenty of time for all that. Get some rest." Charlotte pulled me in for a second hug, squeezing me extra hard this time.

After we parted, Duke and I walked down the steps, waving one last time before turning down the path to the guest house. We walked in silence, which should have been awkward after the day of banter we'd just had. But for some reason, it wasn't. It felt comfortable, familiar, even. When we reached the door to my place, we paused to face each other, and what happened next felt as natural as the multitude of stars scattered across the wide-open sky above us.

"I've never seen this many stars," I breathed, tipping my head back to admire the dazzling display above us.

"Pretty damn beautiful," Duke replied. But when my eyes met his, I saw that he hadn't been looking up at the stars at all. Instead, he was looking at me.

He slipped his hand around the back of my neck, pulling my face to his. Gazing into each other's eyes, our lips only centimeters apart, everything else melted away. The lawsuit, his business, my insistence that we keep things professional. With his hand around my waist and the warmth of his skin against mine, our lips met with surprising tenderness, the exact opposite of what you'd expect after fifteen hours of bickering.

"Sleep well, darlin'," Duke said after pulling away, his fingertips trailing over my wrist as he walked down the steps of the porch, quickly disappearing into the darkness.

"Bye," I breathed, practically floating through the house to my bed.

As I lay there, a small voice in the back of my head kept whispering at me, even as I drifted into a deep, peaceful sleep.

You're in deep shit, pendeja. Deep, deep shit.

Chapter Four

Duke

"I still can't believe that's your signature," Valentina said, tucking the final form of the countersuit in a manila folder as she shook her head.

"What? It's efficient."

"It's illegible."

Reaching across the kitchen table, I pulled the form back out and pointed to my John Hancock.

"Look, you can clearly see a big ole D and a big ole W. The rest you can use your imagination for."

"I'm sure it takes all kinds of imagination to call your D big." Her pretty full lips curved up into a smirk.

I paused, my own mouth twisting into a smile. "Oh, don't worry, darlin', you won't have to use your imagination for much longer."

Valentina froze, a faint blush creeping over her cheeks as she narrowed her eyes at me. "Duke, we talked about this."

I raised my hands in surrender, forcing an innocent look on my face. "I know, I know. Strictly by the books."

Strictly by the books, my ass.

Valentina seemed to be conveniently forgetting the kiss we shared the other night. We hadn't talked about it since, but that kiss was all the confirmation I needed. She was into me, whether she liked it or not. And I wasn't about to let a beautiful woman like her slip through my fingers without something more.

"Now that all the paperwork is handled, what do you say you and I go celebrate? My treat."

Valentina shrugged. "I suppose it couldn't hurt to cut loose a little bit."

"That's what I like to hear."

She rose to her feet. "Just let me run back to the guest house and get changed. Something tells me a pantsuit isn't the right look for a night out in Shady Grove."

* * * *

Twenty minutes later, I pulled up in front of the guest house to find Valentina sitting on the steps of the front porch. Wearing high-waisted skinny jeans and a low-cut pale-yellow top, she was definitely worth the wait.

Damn. The girl had curves.

As she climbed into the passenger seat of my truck, I let out a low whistle.

"Look at you, city-slicker. If I didn't know any better, I'd say you were dressing up for me." I cocked my head in her direction, arching a playful brow.

"What makes you think any of this is for you? From what I've heard, there are plenty of eligible bachelors in this one-horse town."

"That may be, but there's only one Duke Wilder."

She rolled her eyes. "Let's hope so."

When we arrived at the Drunk Skunk, I led Valentina to two open stools at the end of the bar, my favorite seat in the house.

"What can I get you?" I asked, flagging the bartender down.

"I think it's about time I tried that Wilder Whiskey I've been working so hard to protect these last few days."

She leaned her elbows on the bar, revealing even more of her already ample cleavage. I felt a familiar twinge in my gut as I took the sight of her in for the second time that night. The pale yellow contrasted perfectly with her tan skin, her long, dark curls cascading over her shoulders. For a split second, the dim light of the bar caught her eyes just right, and I could have sworn the look she was giving me was almost...sweet.

"You heard the lady," I said, nodding to the bartender.

"Two Wilders, coming right up."

The bartender quickly returned with our drinks. We clinked glasses and took a sip, the appreciative look on Valentina's face bringing a smile to mine.

"I'm not normally a whiskey girl, but I think I can make an exception for this one."

"Let me guess, your go-to is vodka soda."

Valentina shook her head.

"Tequila. Straight."

"I'm impressed."

"But only the good stuff. I need to make my ancestors proud."

"Where are they from?"

"My grandparents immigrated from Mexico right after they got married. My mom was born in LA, and we've lived there ever since. I still have a lot of family in Mexico, though."

"And your dad?"

She rolled her eyes. "He wasn't around much. My mom and grandma raised me, really."

"I'm sorry. Didn't mean to pry."

"No, it's fine," she said, taking a sip of her whiskey. "It's old news by this point."

"Well, if it makes you feel any better, my dad was wasn't around much either. Drank himself to death, but not before running Wilder Whiskey right into the fucking ground."

Valentina stiffened slightly, but I waved a hand to comfort her.

"Old news on this end too, darlin'."

She nodded, tipping her head back and downing the rest of her drink. Waving the bartender over, she ordered another round, eyeing the liquid remaining in my glass. With a smirk, I downed the rest of my drink too, just in time for our tequila shots to arrive.

"You sure about this?" I asked, raising my eyebrows.

"We're supposed to be celebrating, aren't we?"

Two shots and three rounds of banter later, Valentina slid off her stool, smacking my arm with the back of her hand.

"Ay, *pendejo*, come dance with me," she said, taking my hand as she swayed her hips to the twang of country music blasting from the speakers.

How the hell am I supposed to say no to that?

Following her onto the dance floor, I let my hand drop

from hers as she lifted her arms over her head, her body gyrating in a way I'd only seen in music videos. Watching it happen in person was ten times sexier.

I did my best to keep up, but my small-town country boy moves were no match for her Latin roots. The liquor loosened both of us up, and no matter where the music took her, she kept coming back to me. And trust me, just about every pair of eyes in that shithole was watching her. She could have had any man she wanted.

And it felt damn good watching her choose me.

The music slowed, and Valentina brought her body close to mine, looping her arms around my neck. Placing my hands loosely on her hips, I finally took the lead, guiding our movements in time to the country song playing on the speakers. Feeling her body against mine, even to a song this slow, brought me right back to that night we kissed, how much it killed me to leave her when I wanted so much more. She rested her head on my shoulder, the sweet, citrusy scent of her hair making my desire for her skyrocket.

I just needed to make sure she wanted me too.

Dipping my chin, I brought my lips to her ear.

"Wanna get out of here?"

She raised her head and nodded, a small smile spreading across her lips.

I pulled her in for a quick kiss before leading her to the truck. She might have been warned about my "ways," but I wasn't about to show her my hand. Not on the dance floor of a shitty bar.

When we pulled into my driveway, I led Valentina to the front porch, my favorite part of my new place. The moon was full that night, the silvery light playing with her dark hair.

"Charlotte said you built this place yourself after they got married. Is that true?"

"Well, I had a full crew helping me out, but yes, the design and some of the craftsmanship are all me."

She wandered to the far end of the porch, her fingertips trailing over the wooden supports I'd shaped and sanded by hand. I stood by the doorway watching her, my head swimming with all the things I wanted to do to her.

Lifting herself onto the porch railing, she beckoned me toward her with her index finger. I closed the distance between us, taking her jaw in my hands and crushing her mouth against mine. She melted into me, wrapping her legs around my waist, her tongue wrestling mine for control. It was hot—too hot, almost. All the passion, all the tension that had been building between us since the moment I found her in my kitchen? We were finally letting it out, taking it out on each other in the most satisfying way possible.

Well, maybe not the *most* satisfying. Not yet, at least.

Valentina clawed at my chest as I brought my hands to her hips, carrying her from the railing and through the front door without missing a beat. With every step, my cock pressed into her belly, growing harder by the second. Once inside, I pressed her up against the wall, hands still gripping her ass as I descended on her neck, licking and nibbling her delicate skin until she quivered under my tongue.

With her feet finally on the floor, Valentina ground her pelvis against my thigh, her long fingernails raking through my hair. I slipped a hand under her shirt, quickly unclasping her bra before cupping her breast and pinching her nipple between my thumb and forefinger. She gasped at the unexpected sensation, throwing her head back and exposing even more of her neck to me. Massaging her breast with one hand, the other moved to her waist, undoing the button of her jeans. Before moving any further, I paused, pulling back to look her in the eye.

"Is this okay?"

Valentina smirked. "Of course you're a gentleman when it comes down to it."

"Just because I'm country doesn't mean I'm trash. You'd think a city girl like yourself would know—"

Before I could finish, Valentina took my hand and guided it inside her jeans, slipping my fingers beneath her panties.

"Shut up and touch me."

Where the fuck have you been all my life?

She didn't need to tell me twice.

Dipping a finger between her folds, I circled her stiff bud as she writhed against me, her hips bucking in time with my motions. She bit into my neck as I touched her, until her knees trembled, the only sound coming out of her mouth my name.

"Duke..." she breathed into me, snaking her hands under my shirt, her fingernails digging into my skin.

I pressed another finger inside her, and she came moments later, her whole body tensing around me as waves of pleasure washed over her.

When her breathing steadied, she reached for my jeans, her hands quickly finding the rock-hard bulge behind my zipper.

"Not here," I said, lifting and carrying her to my

bedroom.

When I set her down by the bed, we started ripping at each other's clothes until everything was off and both of our chests were heaving in anticipation. Valentina's eyes grew wide at the sight of my cock, all nine inches springing straight up to greet her.

"Think you can handle it?" I took a step toward her, my cock bouncing against my abs.

"You should be asking yourself the same question," she replied, closing the distance between us and stroking the length of my shaft with one long pull.

I shuddered at her touch, a low groan escaping my lips. She stroked again, and our mouths collided, crashing together even more intensely than before. Valentina was good, but she had no idea what was in store for her.

I walked her backward until her legs hit the bed and pushed her onto her back. Within moments, my tongue was circling her clit, and Valentina took a fistful of my comforter in each hand to brace herself.

"Fuck, darlin', you taste even better than I imagined," I growled between laps as her hips bucked against me. She moaned in response, her body shaking as I brought her to a second orgasm with my tongue.

When she finally caught her breath, I pulled a rubber out of the drawer in the bedside table, rolling it over my length and aligning my hips with Valentina's. She spread her legs wide for me, her eyes still hungry, even after the pleasure I'd already given her. She was insatiable, and it only made me want to pound her pretty little pussy until she couldn't take it anymore.

I pushed my tip into her hot, wet center, slowly at first, watching her face as she took me in. With her head tilted back, her mouth gaped open, a low guttural moan coming deep from within her. I buried myself fully inside her, wasting no time in finding our rhythm. With every move my need for her intensified, the ache deep inside me only growing stronger. Her breasts bounced with the movement. I pumped harder and harder until I collapsed on top of her, pleasure exploding from within me in wave after wave, her tight channel clenched and pulsing around me.

As the waves subsided, I rolled over onto my back, sweat beading along my forehead. I was totally spent. When I turned to Valentina, I swear the look on her face said she could go for at least three more rounds. I chuckled and shook my head.

This woman might be the best thing to ever happen to me.
Either that, or the worst.

Chapter Five

Valentina

I woke up to sunlight streaming through the window, one of the oak trees in the yard casting a long shadow on the hardwood floor. I rolled over to check the time, only to be confronted with a tousle of brown hair attached to a very muscular, very attractive shirtless body. The tousle turned to me, its green eyes fluttering open, an adorably dimpled smile spreading across its face.

Oh fuck.

"Well, aren't you a pretty sight to see first thing in the morning."

Fuck, fuck, fuck.

Clapping a hand over my mouth, I immediately sat up, my head spinning as the realization of what happened last night washed over me. The bar…the whiskey…the dancing…the porch…and Duke Wilder inside me, rocking my world to its core.

"I, uh, I have to go," I muttered, swinging my legs over the side of the bed and quickly scanning the room for my clothes. My jeans were in the corner, my top and bra right next to them. *Where are my fucking panties?*

"Are you sure you don't have time for round four? Or would that make it five?" Duke drawled, propping himself up on his side with one elbow, the gray cotton sheet slipping from his waist.

Quickly clasping my bra and slipping the straps over my shoulders, I threw my top over my head, covering myself with my jeans while I kept searching for my missing underwear.

"Last night was a mistake," I said, purposefully avoiding eye contact with Duke. Or with his dick. His thick, nine-inch, magic dick, which apparently had the power to make me throw all common sense out the window.

"Wait, hold on, what do you mean a mistake?"

"*Gracias a Dios*," I said as my fingers landed on the thin lacy fabric of my panties, which had somehow ended up under the bed. After pulling them on, I turned to tell Duke off, but the look on his face caught me off guard. Any trace of cockiness was gone, and if I didn't know any better, I'd almost say he looked sincere.

"I don't want you to regret what happened. We're adults, and we deserve to have a little fun."

He stepped into a pair of boxer briefs and sat on the edge of the bed, the outline of his manhood in the stretchy cotton sending my mind to the first day we met. In some ways, it felt like we'd come a long way since then. But then again, there I was, half-naked in his bedroom, just like he'd wanted.

But if I'm being honest? Just like I'd wanted, too.

I sighed and sat on the bed next to him.

"But I'm going back to LA soon." *Not to mention*

Charlotte will have a fucking heyday when she finds out about this.

"I know. But that doesn't mean we can't enjoy each other while you're here."

I crossed one leg over the other, already aware of the soreness in those tiny thigh muscles that hadn't been used in a while. As much as I didn't want to admit it, Duke lived up to his reputation.

And then some.

Jesus, the man was an animal in bed.

"What do you have in mind?"

Duke smiled, his lip curling into that stupid half-smirk that made me want to slap him and dry hump him at the same time.

"You have a bathing suit? Go get changed. I'll pick you up in a little while."

* * * *

Half an hour later, Duke's truck pulled up the driveway. My stomach did a backflip at the thought of him in a pair of swim trunks. Not that his six pack was a surprise by this point. But that didn't mean I wasn't excited for the show.

I adjusted the strap of my baby blue bikini, tucking it under my tank top. I was grateful in that moment for my over-packing tendencies. Charlotte hadn't said anything about swimming, but I'd figured it couldn't hurt to be prepared. Thank God for intuition.

As I climbed into the passenger seat, Duke jerked his head to a picnic basket at my feet.

"Careful, darlin', you don't want to crush our lunch."

"Lunch? Where are we going?"

"You'll see. And no peeking," he said, arching a brow as I leaned down to lift the lid. "I was hoping we could leave one last thing to the imagination."

I sat up straight, raising my hands in surrender.

"I didn't take you for the modest type."

"There's a lot about me you still have to learn."

With that, Duke turned up the radio, country music filling the truck. Normally, I would have rolled my eyes at that twangy stuff, but as we turned down a dirt road, Duke's taste in music seemed weirdly perfect. The trees outside my window were unlike anything I'd seen in LA. All the Texas greenery and plant life made the lonely palm trees back home look like sad Hollywood excuses for nature.

We came to a stop at what seemed like the middle of nowhere. Surrounded by more trees and bushes I'd never seen before, the spot was beautiful, sure, but not exactly what I'd imagined our picnic getaway location would look like.

"Is this it?" I asked as Duke put the car in park.

He smiled and shook his head.

"Follow me."

With the picnic basket in one hand, he took mine in the other, weaving through trees and pushing shrubs aside as we went. We weren't following any path I could see, so I had no idea how he knew where to go, but by that point, I wasn't worried. My mom had always warned me about letting strange men take me places, but Duke wasn't a stranger anymore. I didn't know it until that moment, but as I followed him blindly to what looked like the middle of nowhere, it hit me like a ton of bricks:

I trusted him.

Even if that made me like every other doe-eyed sucker who fell for him.

Duke pushed past some thick leafy bushes, revealing a clearing unlike anything I'd ever seen before. The dirt beneath our feet led to a small sandy beach and water bluer and clearer than I thought possible. A stream poured into the swimming hole from between two huge rock formations dotted with giant leafy trees, making it feel like we'd entered a whole other world.

"Welcome to the best kept secret in all of Shady Grove," Duke said, setting the picnic basket down and admiring the view.

"How is this place even real?"

I could barely keep my mouth from gaping open as I took it all in. From the sound of the stream flowing into the reserve to the trill of the birds across the way, that place was like something out of a fairy tale. I even saw a few magical-looking dragonflies skimming the surface of the water.

"Our parents used to take us here when we were little, before everything went south. Some of my best memories as a kid happened here."

"And I thought Six Flags was cool growing up."

Duke peeled off his T-shirt and tossed it by the basket, climbing onto one of the rocks and turning to wink at me.

"Are you coming or what?"

Without waiting for me to answer, he dove into the deepest part of the water. Part of me wished he would have stood a little longer on the rock so I had more time to admire his rippling back muscles, but I knew there'd be time for that later. Shedding my shorts and tank top, I walked to the water, yelping when my toes reached the edge.

"It's freezing!"

"This is all-natural spring water, darlin'," Duke said when he resurfaced. "Sixty-eight degrees year-round."

I shuddered as I stepped deeper into the water, submerging my feet and calves.

"At this rate, you'll barely get your head underwater by sunset," Duke said, splashing water in my direction.

"Shut up." I kept walking until the water came up to my waist, sending a spray of water into Duke's face.

"Make me."

He flashed that devilish smile of his and dove under, popping up a few feet to my left. I smiled and swam after him, loving the way the cold water made me feel like a kid again. We kept on like that for a while, chasing each other around the swimming hole, splashing and teasing and laughing until our limbs were tired and our stomachs started to growl. We swam ashore, where Duke spread out a picnic blanket, and we ate the meat, cheese, and fruit plate he'd packed for us. He'd even managed to slip a few beers in there—a couple IPAs for him, and something a little more drinkable for me.

Everything about the day was perfect, from the surprise of the swimming hole to Duke's lips against my skin after lunch. I thought I'd been on good dates before, but this was something else. I'd never had a man plan something like that for me, taking me somewhere I'd never been, showing me a part of his world.

As we lay on the blanket, lips tired and sore from kissing, the Texas sun warming our skin, just one thought kept crossing my mind.

Why can't guys like this exist in LA?

"Get your pretty little ass over here, I'm not done with you yet." Duke smirked, heading straight for me with a determined expression, and my belly flipped.

Chapter Six

Duke

I couldn't tell if I was drunk on whiskey or drunk on her, but either way, my world was soaked in a slap-happy haze, and I was fucking loving it.

When I'd dropped Valentina off at the guest house after our day at the swimming hole, my lips almost swollen from making out, I'd texted to see if she wanted to meet for a drink later, and she was quick to accept. Watching a huge smile erupt across her face as we played and splashed in the water meant more to me than I'd realized, and even though we'd spent the entire day together, I couldn't wait another day to see her again.

We met up at the Drunk Skunk, her hair still a little damp from the shower. I got the first round as a thank you for not jumping out of the car when I'd turned down that first dirt road. Valentina got the second as a thank you for not murdering her and throwing her body in the spring water.

"I've watched enough true crime shows to know how that story would have ended," she said, her lip curling into a smile.

"With me in my pick-up, halfway to Canada?"

She shook her head. "You'd have a whole band of angry Mexicans waiting for you at the border to take their revenge."

We both laughed, whiskey burning my sinuses as I almost snorted it through my nose. For as much time as we'd spent together in the past week, Valentina's wit was still sharp enough to catch me off guard.

But I also couldn't believe it had only been a week. Sitting across from her, my whiskey on her lips, an easy, relaxed smile on her face, it all felt so natural. Like she'd lived in Shady Grove her whole life. Like she belonged there. With me.

"If I didn't know any better, I'd say you were starting to warm up to this little town," I said, dipping my chin and swirling the liquid in my tumbler.

"I don't know. If I don't drive through a Starbucks soon, I might lose my license as a city girl," she replied, arching a perfectly sculpted brow my way.

I smiled and shook my head. Valentina tossed back the rest of her drink, her glossy black hair shimmering over her shoulders. Even in the dim lighting of the bar, she was radiant. Her low-cut top cupped her perky breasts just right, and her jeans hugged her hips in all the right places. The whiskey made her brown eyes glitter, her full lips boasting just a hint of gloss. Sure, she could sometimes be a pain in the ass, but I couldn't deny how much I enjoyed having her next to me.

"Could you ever see yourself leaving the city for some place quieter? Some place like this?"

I regretted it the second I said it. Cringed at how needy it sounded. I wasn't the kind of man who kept women around for longer than a few lays, and I especially wasn't the kind of man to ask a woman to move across state lines to be with him. Every muscle in my body tensed as I waited for whatever biting remark Valentina was about to throw my way.

Only she didn't.

"Honestly? I never thought I'd want anything besides the city hustle, but after these past few days…I think I'm starting to see the appeal of a place like this."

I nodded and finished the last of my drink, shrugging like she'd said something as casual as "I like the color blue." But in reality, my entire world just got rocked. Because what just came out of her mouth opened a whole new door of possibilities. A door I hadn't considered, hadn't even thought existed.

"I'll drink to that," I replied, flagging the bartender down for another round.

Just then some movement over Valentina's shoulder caught my eye. A woman had just walked into the bar, her chin-length, curly brown hair bouncing with every step. Our eyes met, and she smiled like she knew me. I gave her a half smile back, which quickly faded when I realized who she was. Amber, my ex from college who'd moved away shortly after we graduated. Her hair was different, but her face was pretty much the same. The same round cheeks, full lips, pale blue eyes. Eyes that bore into mine as she turned the corner, making her way to our table.

It was then that I noticed she wasn't alone. She had a boy with her, and when his gaze met mine, my stomach dropped.

That kid could have been my clone.

Brown hair, green eyes, same nose, same chin. He even

had my same damn dimples. My heart was beating so hard, I thought it might jump right out from my throat. *What the hell?*

"Earth to Duke, are you paying for this round, or am I?" Valentina's voice broke me from my panic just in time for Amber and the little boy to reach our table.

"Hey there, Duke. I was hoping I'd find you here." Amber's voice was just as sweet and syrupy as ever, but in that moment, it sounded to me like nails on a chalkboard. She smiled broadly at me, her hands on the boy's shoulders, while the boy stared blankly up at me.

"Hey, Amber," I said when I finally found my voice. "What's it been, ten years?"

"Almost eleven."

I nodded, my mind still spinning, and that's when I noticed Valentina. She was sitting up perfectly straight, her lips pulled into a thin, taut line across her face. Her eyes were wide and trained on the boy's face, her expression unreadable.

"This is Valentina," I said, gesturing to her, but the moment the words left my mouth, Valentina stood and grabbed her purse.

"I was just leaving," she said, quickly tucking her chair in behind her and forcing a smile at Amber and the boy.

"Valentina—"

I stood to stop her, but she was already gone. Every eye in the Drunk Skunk was on me and my new mini-me. Guessing it wasn't just me noticing the uncanny resemblance. Chasing my new flame out the door would have been a surefire way of making front-page gossip news. So sadly, I let Valentina go with a promise to myself to call her later.

Amber cleared her throat, and I smiled weakly at her. "What brings you into town?"

"Well, me and Payton here are on a little road trip. I thought it might be nice to finally show him where I grew up."

I looked down at Payton, smiling and trying to treat him like I would treat any new kid I met. "Hey there, Payton. How do you like Shady Grove so far?"

"It's alright. Not a whole lot to do here."

"Yeah, I bet it's pretty different from where you're from. Still living in San Antonio?" I asked Amber.

She shook her head. "I moved to Houston ten years ago. Right after Payton was born."

Ten years. The math added up. Payton could definitely be my kid.

Fuck.

"Good for you guys. Do you like Houston, buddy?"

Payton nodded, but it was clear he was getting restless. He shrugged his mother's hands off of him, and Amber smiled knowingly at me.

"I better get him back to the hotel. We're staying at the Willow Inn, and Opal said something about bringing cookies for Payton before bed."

"Well, I'm glad we ran into each other. Maybe I'll see you guys around."

Amber smiled, and the two of them walked away, greeting a few other old friends before leaving. I felt my entire body relax the moment they left, like I'd been holding myself together the entire time I was in their presence.

I downed my whiskey in one gulp, racking my brain to

remember those last few months of my relationship with Amber. But there was just one thought that kept circling my mind.

Was I really that much of an idiot at nineteen?

Chapter Seven

Valentina

"Maybe it's not what you think." Charlotte was sitting on my bed, glass of red wine in hand, watching me pack my things with those worried eyes of hers.

I threw my still-damp bathing suit into the suitcase, stuffing the memories of our day at the swimming hole into a deep, dark corner in my mind.

"You didn't see that little boy, Char. He was the spitting image of Duke. There's no way he's not his kid."

And there's no way in hell I'm sticking around long enough to find out.

It was stupid getting involved with Duke in the first place. His whole life was here—an entire history I didn't understand. And my life was in LA. It was as simple as that. He didn't owe me explanations about his exes, or the fact that he had a kid I knew nothing about.

"I just think that it might be worth talking to him about it.

Maybe running back to California all angry and broken isn't the best way of going about things."

Puta madre. I always hated it when she was right.

But that didn't mean I had to listen to her.

"I didn't *fall* for him. We fucked one time. And besides, what am I going to do, pick up my life and move to the middle of nowhere for a good lay?"

Charlotte winced, and I immediately felt like shit. I guess that's kinda what she did. Only Luke and her are the real deal—totally in love and all that shit. Things never had the chance to get that far between Duke and me. Tossing the pair of jeans I'd been folding onto the growing pile in my suitcase, I joined her on the bed, placing my hand on hers.

"Look, I'm sorry, I didn't mean that. You and Luke are great. I'm just...I'm so embarrassed. I can't believe I let myself get involved with Duke, even after you warned me about him. And oh my God, Char, I don't know how you deal with the freaking gossip in this town. I swear they even turned off the music to eavesdrop on us the second his ex walked up to the bar."

She laughed, shrugging and downing the last of her wine.

"You get used to it. Molly didn't say anything about the music stopping, but she did mention that the whole town thinks the kid is Duke's too."

"You mean he didn't even know about the kid?"

Charlotte shook her head. "Amber never said a word."

Wow. That's a hell of a lot to deal with.

"*Qué pinche culero*," I muttered. I laid back on the bed with a huff, a tension headache already forming at the base of my skull. All I wanted was to be back in my apartment, soaking in the clawfoot tub I saved up for six months to splurge on, a thousand miles away from my problems.

Charlotte flopped down on the bed next to me, our heads sinking into the fluffy blue comforter.

"Are you sure you have to go back? I feel like you just got here."

A familiar sting welled in the corners of my eyes. I'd been so wrapped up with Duke these past few days, I'd barely spent any time with my best friend. And now I was leaving because of him too? I hated the way he affected me so much, hated how his stupid, arrogant, beautiful face made everything feel so messy and complicated.

But I knew that if I stayed, it would only make things worse. Clearly, he wasn't in a position to be seeing anyone new. Not if he had a kid he was just finding out about. There was only one thing left to do.

No matter how much it broke me to do it.

"You and Luke can always come to LA," I said, rolling over onto my side.

Charlotte mirrored my position, propping her head up on her wrist.

"We were already talking about flying out to see you in the fall."

That did me in. Tears fell freely down my cheeks, half out of love for my best friend and half out of heartbreak over Duke. I didn't want to admit it, but I had fallen for him, whether I wanted to or not.

And that was why I knew I couldn't stay. I had a great job at a successful law firm in California. My family was there. I had a lease on an apartment. In the real world, you didn't just ride off into the sunset for some hot country guy. No matter how nice his biceps were.

But Charlotte was still frowning at me.

"I just think Duke is better off working it out with his ex. It looks like they have a lot to catch up on, and I don't want to make him choose between a woman he hardly knows and the family he didn't know he had."

Charlotte nodded, tears welling up in her eyes as well. She pulled me in for a hug, rubbing my back like she always did when some *pendejo* broke my heart. She'd always been there for me, no matter what, and in that moment more than ever, I was grateful for my friend.

Her phone chimed, and when she checked it, a nervous smile spread across her face.

"So, don't be mad, but Molly's here. She's the one driving you to the airport."

Okay, scratch what I said about being grateful for her. I knew Molly was Duke's younger sister, even if I hadn't formally met her yet.

I sat up, a mixture of confusion and frustration brewing between my brows.

"Why Molly? I haven't even met her yet."

"I know, I know! But look, she was planning to drive into the city today, and once you booked your flight for this evening, it didn't make sense to drive you out myself if she was already going."

"You've got to be kidding me."

"Besides, she wanted to finally meet the woman with a mouth that could shut her big-mouthed brother up."

I snorted, warmth spreading over my cheeks. *Is that really what people have been saying about me?*

"Ugh, fine, I'll ride with the little sister. Is there anything I need to know before I meet her? Not that your warnings have done much good in the past."

Charlotte rolled her eyes. "Molly's an absolute sweetheart. She can just be a little…protective of her brothers sometimes. But it comes from a good place. She has a good heart."

"Oh, great, so I'm about to spend the next hour in the car with someone who hates my guts."

"Not necessarily. She just wants to meet you for herself."

Twenty minutes, three more rounds of hugs, and a fresh batch of tears later, I was sitting shotgun in Molly's pickup truck, desperately trying to think of something to talk about. The sky seemed to know how I was feeling, its normal perfect shade of blue quickly turning dark gray with huge, heavy-looking clouds moving right toward us. Fantastic.

"Looks like you guys have some crazy weather headed your way," I said. *Am I really resorting to talking about the weather? Fuck me.*

"I bet you're pretty happy to be on your way back to LA right about now," Molly replied. Her voice was light and friendly, but I could smell a gossip from a mile away. She was testing me, trying to suss out how I felt about her brother. *Game on.* Bring it, baby.

"It'll be nice to stop living out of a suitcase, but I enjoyed Shady Grove more than I expected to."

"Oh?" Molly's ears practically perked up, ready for me to spill something about Duke.

"Sure. The bar's dirt cheap, the food is swimming in butter, and my best friend lives here. Plus, your brother showed me that swimming hole, and I can guarantee there's nothing like that place in LA."

She stiffened, her eyes growing wide.

"Duke took you to our spot? The place through the woods off the backroads?"

I nodded, studying her face as she processed the news. She didn't look upset. It was more like she was surprised. Shocked, even.

"None of us have been back there since..." She trailed off, clearly lost in thought.

I was about to ask her what was wrong when a huge bolt of lightning struck way too close to us, immediately followed by the loudest crack of thunder I'd ever heard. Molly and I both yelped, the pickup swerving slightly before she corrected course. Heavy rain poured down on us out of nowhere, the wind aiming the drops directly at the windshield. Even on full blast, the wipers didn't stand a chance, water totally obscured our line of sight. I definitely wasn't in California anymore.

"We have to pull over," Molly said, her voice straining over the downpour.

I groaned.

"But my flight leaves in an hour."

"Trust me, that plane's not going anywhere."

Shit. She was probably right.

As if on cue, my phone chimed with the notification that all flights out of the local airport were cancelled. Leaning back into the headrest, I took a deep breath to try to calm down. *Can't just one thing go right on this* pinche *trip?!*

We rolled to a stop on the side of the road, the only car on the highway for miles. While Molly frantically typed on her phone, I pressed my forehead to the cool glass of the window, watching lightning flash around us, the thunder shaking the whole car.

I guess Mother Nature doesn't want me to leave either.

Chapter Eight

Duke

My phone buzzed in the back pocket of my jeans as a crack of thunder rumbled through the house. My place was totally dark and I didn't bother turning on a light—the darkness matched my mood perfectly right now.

I closed the door to the refrigerator, the glass bottles of the six pack I'd just bought clinking against each other. I pulled my phone out and leaned against the counter, brows furrowed in confusion. The text was from my sister. My sister who was supposed to be halfway down the highway right about now. My sister who never texted while driving.

Storm is too bad—had to pull over.

A second text rolled in. A text that changed everything.

Valentina's flight is cancelled.

I quickly texted her back, moving my thumbs as fast as they would go.

Where are you?

She replied that they were fine, but pulled over in a wide shoulder, waiting for the storm to pass, or at least let up enough for them to drive again. I shot Molly another text, my stomach sinking.

I'm sure Valentina's pretty upset about her flight.

When she'd stormed out of the bar the other night, I knew she was walking out of my life forever. Somehow, I just knew. I always knew a girl like her, classy, smart, and beautiful didn't belong with a redneck like me. Sure I could fix her car with my own two hands, start a campfire, or catch her a fish for dinner, but I didn't know shit about fine wines or art. And as much as it stung to watch her leave, I couldn't blame her. Who would want to be with a man who had a ten-year-old son he'd never met?

Why don't you come down here and give her a reason to stay?

Molly's text took me aback. It wasn't like her to encourage me to date anyone, let alone someone she barely knew.

I'm not sure that's a good idea.

Duke, she told me about the swimming hole. Don't pretend you don't have feelings for her.

She was right. I'd played it cool when I took her there, but Valentina was the first person outside my family who'd seen our spot. I didn't know why at the time, but some instinctual part of me wanted to take her there. But now that she was leaving, I understood. Being around her changed me. She tapped into a side of me I didn't think was there, opened something in me I didn't think I'd ever have. Fuck, she split my chest wide open somehow in those few short days, and I already felt the pangs of her departure.

That's when I knew for sure.

There was no way in hell I was letting her go. I still had no clue what would happen with Amber and Payton, but I knew I couldn't lose Valentina.

The second Molly sent me their exact location, I grabbed my keys and got in my truck. The rain beat down on the windshield as I drove to the highway, lightning striking on the horizon. A storm like that hadn't come through Shady Grove in years. Molly wasn't a bad driver, but I was glad she'd pulled over. Because even with my windshield wipers on full tilt, I was having a hard time seeing the road ahead of me.

Lucky for me, Molly and Valentina hadn't gotten far, and just ten minutes later, I pulled up behind them on the shoulder, my headlights flooding the backseat. The rain was pouring harder than ever, but at that point, I didn't care. I had to see her, had to talk to her, had to let her know how I felt.

I climbed out of my truck and jogged the few short yards between our cars, yanking the backseat door open and tumbling in. Valentina cursed loudly in Spanish, turning and looking like she was ready to smack me all the way to next Tuesday.

Somehow, I even loved that. She was feisty as hell, and it only made me smile.

"Relax, baby. It's Duke," I said, raising my hands in surrender.

"*Puta madre, pendejo*, what is your problem?!" Valentina shouted, chest heaving, eyes wild.

"I think that's my bad," Molly said, pulling her lips into a tight, apologetic smile. "I should have told you he was coming."

"You think?!"

"Warning or not, I'm here now. And darlin', you and I have to talk."

Valentina rolled her eyes, muttering more Spanish curse

words under her breath. Molly whistled through her teeth, shifting her eyes out the window.

"I, uh…I'll give you two some space," she said, reaching for her door.

"No, I'll go," Valentina said, grabbing my keys and climbing out into the rain, slamming the door closed behind her.

I immediately followed right behind her, exiting the car and closing the distance between us in two strides. It was pouring so hard that we were both soaked in seconds, my gray T-shirt sticking to my skin.

"What could you possibly want?" Valentina asked, crossing her arms and squaring her shoulders at me.

"Isn't it obvious?"

Lightning flashed, and for a brief moment, I could see her expression clearly. Surprise. Pain. Frustration. A hint of anger. And somewhere deep inside there, something softer, more tender.

"No, Duke, in this situation, what you want from me is the one thing that isn't obvious."

"I probably deserve that. But goddammit, woman, do you have to make this so hard?"

Her eyes grew wide, and she threw her hands up in the air. "What the fuck are you talking about?"

"You, Valentina. I'm talking about you."

She paused, her hands slowly lowering to her sides. "What do you—"

"I want you, you crazy, sassy woman. More than anything else. I didn't realize it until you were about to leave my life forever, but I've fallen for you, and the last thing I want you to do is leave."

I paused to take a breath, shoving the wet hair plastered to my forehead out of my face.

"Even if it turns out I'm a father."

"Duke, I don't know…"

"You don't have to make a decision now. Just please, don't leave yet. I'm meeting with Amber tonight to talk about what's going on. Don't throw this away over something that might not even be true."

She sighed, bringing her hands to her forehead and rubbing her temples. The rain was finally starting to let up, a few small patches of sunlight appearing around us. Further down the highway, the storm raged on, continuing its course through the sky.

"Fine. We can talk in the morning. But that doesn't mean I'm not getting on the first flight out of here once your *pinche pequeño* airport opens back up."

"Fair enough, darlin'."

A smile erupted on my face, but Valentina only half-smiled back. She had every right to be cautious, and I totally understood why she felt that way. But as for me? I had a little bit of hope. Hope that she might stick around, that we might get a chance to let this crazy, awesome, infuriating-as-hell thing between us grow.

And in that moment, that hope was all I needed.

* * * *

That night, I walked into the Drunk Skunk to find Amber waiting for me at a high-top table by the windows. Originally, she wanted to meet for dinner, but drinks made it a little more casual. Plus, I had no idea what kind of news I was about to receive, and it was probably best to have a whole lot of whiskey nearby.

Every eye in the room was on me as I walked over to her, and I smiled when she looked up and noticed me. She smiled back, and the warmth in her pale blue eyes took me right back to all those years ago when this place used to be our spot. We'd plant ourselves in the middle of the bar and get rip-roaring drunk, ending the night by hopping in the bed of my rusty old pickup and knocking boots 'til the cops came to kick us out.

It's safe to say that I've matured since then. Or I've just learned how not to get caught having public sex. Take your pick. Good thing the local sheriff is a buddy of mine from high school.

"Hey there, Duke. I ordered us a couple glasses of your whiskey. I hope that's okay." Amber pulled me in for a hug, her perfume more floral than it was when I knew her.

"If I wouldn't drink it, I wouldn't sell it."

I sat down across from her, taking a good look at her face for the first time since she surprised me last night. She had a faint shadow under her eyes and a small, shallow line between her brows that deepened when she smiled. When she tucked her hair behind her ear, I noticed a few gray hairs coming in around her temples. She didn't look bad—she was still as good-looking as ever—but it was clear those last ten years had done a number on her.

Makes sense if she's been raising a child all on her own.

We clinked glasses and took a sip, an impressed smile

forming on Amber's face as the whiskey hit her tongue.

"I've got to be honest, I was expecting this to taste like shit."

We laughed and some of the awkward tension between us lessened. I leaned my elbows on the table, shrugging and rubbing my neck.

"It hasn't been easy. But me and Luke worked our asses off to turn that distillery into something we could be proud of."

"Well, it paid off. I knew you had it in you. It was always just a matter of everything else lining up right."

"That means a lot coming from you. I appreciate it."

She nodded, and when we smiled at each other, for a moment, it felt like everything was normal. Like we were just a couple of old friends catching up. Like she didn't have a son who might or might not be biologically mine. I decided to proceed with caution.

"Where's Payton hanging out tonight?"

"With Opal. I think they're having a movie marathon or something like that. She's really taken to him."

"Yep, that sounds like Opal. She was always doing nice things for my brother and me when we were kids."

"Yeah, she mentioned that. She also told me about all the rumors spreading around since Payton and I saw you last night. About you being his father."

A pit formed in my stomach, and I folded my hands on the table in front of me. I guess we were doing this now.

"I've been wondering about that too. The math adds up. I just can't believe you didn't tell me."

Amber paused, her lip curling at the edge. "You're joking,

right?"

I froze and slowly shook my head.

She laughed—harder and louder than seemed appropriate for the situation, causing the whole room to turn and look at us. I forced a nervous, weak smile, nodding at the people closest to us like everything was normal. Meanwhile, Amber continued laughing, fits of giggles rolling through her as she placed a hand on her chest and dabbed tears out of the corners of her eyes.

What the hell is going on?

When she saw the look on my face, she clapped a hand over her mouth, her brows knit together in apology.

"I'm so sorry, I'm not trying to make fun of you. It's just, you were the *most* careful guy when we were together. Always made sure I took my birth control. Always used a rubber, no matter how plastered we were in your truck. You didn't want anything getting in the way of you turning your dad's piss-tillery around, especially not a baby and a shotgun wedding. Do you really not remember any of that?"

I stared at her dumbfounded, mouth hanging open. Guess I wasn't as much of an idiot ten years ago as I thought. Thank God, but this still didn't add up.

"I'm not sure what to say. He looks so much like me."

She raised her eyebrows and shook her head, smiling like she wasn't surprised in the least.

"Well, breathe easy, Duke Wilder. You're not a father. You can go back to laser-focusing on achieving your goals, back-logged child-support free."

I chuckled, downing my whiskey and ordering another. "Wait a second. If I'm not the father, then who...?"

She took a quick breath in, pulling her lips back over her teeth. "Some guy I barely knew. Out-of-towner just passing through."

She shook her head and stared down at her lap. "Were you ever able to get ahold of him?"

"We didn't exchange numbers. I didn't even know his last name. I won't sugarcoat it, it hasn't been easy. But Payton changed my life, and I can't imagine it without him."

"It's amazing what you've done. Payton seems like a good kid."

"Thanks. I think so."

We both smiled, but my heart sank at the thought of Amber struggling all those years, then bristled at the thought of the asshole who knocked her up. But if anyone in this town understood the appeal of out-of-towners, it was me.

"Can I give you one piece of advice, though? As someone who used to know you pretty well," Amber said, cocking her head to the side.

I shrugged. "Fire away."

"Don't get so laser-focused that you can't see all the other good things around you. I'd hate to see anything else important slip away."

I nodded, my mind already on the next morning. "Oh, don't worry. I won't."

"Thanks for meeting me. It was good to see you again." Amber grinned.

"Likewise. And if you plan on sticking around, let me know. I'd be happy to show Payton how to throw a spiral, or take him fishing or something."

She nodded. "I know he'd like that. Thanks."

Chapter Nine

Valentina

Zipping my suitcase closed, I stood it upright and rolled it by the door. I wasn't planning on taking it to Duke's, but I wanted to be ready to leave as soon as possible, just in case our meeting went south. I had a plane ticket to LA on hold for later that day, and I'd spent the whole morning steeling myself for bad news. Like if Duke was the kind of man to have a ten-year-old son he didn't know about. Like I was the kind of idiot who fell for that kind of man.

I checked my reflection one last time before walking out the door. Black leggings, a soft, cotton V-neck that skimmed my body just right, and my favorite pair of Nike running shoes. I'd made the decision to wear my comfy plane clothes to Duke's as further preparation for the worst. The last thing I wanted was to wind up on a plane wearing a cute-ass outfit I'd just been royally rejected in.

The walk to Duke's felt longer than usual, and as I got

closer, I started to feel lightheaded. My stomach was churning with nerves, a tingly feeling spreading to my toes. *Why am I so nervous?*

I climbed the porch steps slowly, taking deep breaths in and out. One look at the railing sent me right back to that night with Duke. His hands in my hair, his lips on my skin. I shook my head, running my hand on the back of my neck. One more deep breath, then I knocked on the door.

Within seconds, Duke swung it open, and that deep breath I'd just taken blew out of me all at once. He stood there smiling at me, a white T-shirt straining over his muscled chest, those stupid, adorable dimples sending a shock straight to my core. Damn him for being so irresistible. Damn him for making it so much harder to let him go.

"Glad to see you remembered to put clothes on this time," I said as he ushered me in.

"That can change if you want," he replied, his eyes wandering to the tight fabric perfectly hugging my ass.

I narrowed my eyes, and he immediately backed off.

"Right. Too soon for jokes."

As I walked into the kitchen, my mouth dropped open. Every inch of counter space was covered in bouquets of pink dahlias—my favorite—and the table was scattered with my favorite foods and drinks. A huge bottle of top shelf tequila stood tall in the middle, surrounded by freshly-cut pineapple, carnitas tacos with cilantro and onions, a plate of homemade cinnamon rolls, and a basket filled with my favorite snacks and candies. On the edge of the counter was a to-go cup from Starbucks, and based on the markings on the side, I knew it was my order: a non-fat latte with a dash of cinnamon.

"Duke, I...what is all this?"

He smiled, stepping around me, shrugging and stuffing his hands in his pockets.

"Guess I just wanted to give you a few more reasons to stay."

"But—"

"I might have bribed Charlotte into telling me a few of your favorite things." He grinned.

"Duke ..."

"Hold on. Just listen. I know Shady Grove is a far cry from the city. We don't have a wide variety of restaurants or bars, we've got one tiny café that's closed on Sundays, and we're so far in the middle of nowhere that some fruits and vegetables that are commonplace everywhere else seem exotic and rare. But I looked into it, and the nearest Starbucks is only an hour away. And a couple towns over, there's a Mexican place that claims to be authentic. As for the rest of this stuff, I had to do some digging—"

I cut him off with a kiss on the lips, throwing my arms around his neck.

"But what about Amber?"

"Payton isn't mine. She cleared it all up last night."

I kissed him again, this time running my fingers through his hair. He wrapped me in his arms, my body sinking into his broad chest. When we parted, I looked around again, shaking my head at all the things he'd gotten me.

"*Dios mio, cabron*, when did you get all this?"

His proud, dimpled smile made my heart melt.

"Let's just say it was an early morning. Turns out, I'm no good at coring pineapple. That's attempt number two."

"You bought two pineapples?"

"I had a feeling I'd need a spare."

I smiled and shook my head again, bringing the lukewarm latte to my lips. The familiar scent wafted up through my nostrils, a scent that used to bring me comfort and calm on hectic mornings, and on occasion, in the middle of a crazy day. But when the liquid hit my tongue, something about it tasted different. The barista did fine. The order was spot-on.

It was me. I was different. I didn't need the comfort and calm as much as I used to. The country had done that instead. I didn't need the liquid form.

"Everything you ever dreamed of?" Duke asked, amusement on his face.

"Nothing tastes quite as much like corporate America."

He chuckled, a serious look quickly falling over his face.

"Now, I want to be clear, darlin', all this is meant to show you that life here in Shady Grove doesn't have to be all that different from the city. I'm not trying to bribe you into staying. My winning smile and matchless charm already do that for me."

I rolled my eyes, making a face like I was going to be sick. But he was right. I didn't have to stay. Even if he didn't have a ten-year-old son, there was no guarantee that what Duke and I had would last. We barely knew each other, only had sex one time. What if it was all just a fluke? What if the moment I decided to stay, the magic disappeared, and we quickly started to resent each other for the time and energy we were both wasting on a relationship that was never meant to go past a summer fling?

I looked up into his eyes, those two green gems that had

the power to make my blood boil with frustration one second and with lust the next, and I knew that none of that was true. From the moment we met, our dynamic came naturally, the playful energy between us a symptom of the cellular-level connection we had. It was too real, too magic. That was why we insisted on teasing and fighting. Because the idea that soulmates might be real, that love at first sight might exist?

That was scarier than hating each other's guts.

"My firm did just roll out the option of working remotely," I said, slipping my arm around his waist.

Duke beamed down at me, relief and joy radiating from his face.

"And we do have an extra house on the property for you. Before you move in with me, of course."

"What makes you think we wouldn't move into my place? Your place is cute, but just wait 'til you see what I can do with a Home Goods catalog."

"Charlotte let me in on a few of your big-city secrets, darlin'."

"Charlotte seems to be helping you out a lot these days." I arched a brow at the spread on the table, knowing full well I'd only told him about half of these favorites.

"She might have tipped me off about the dahlias," he admitted.

I raised another brow.

"And the pineapple."

I laughed, rubbing his back before returning to the table to take a bite of the fruit. Sweet and tangy, it was fresher than I was expecting. Definitely worth the wild goose chase I'm sure he went on.

"Oh my god, that reminds me. I need to call Charlotte. She's going to freak out that I'm staying."

I reached for my phone, but Duke stopped me, taking my hand and pulling me to him.

"Actually, I had one more thing planned, just in case you decided to stay."

His free hand dropped to my waist, sliding over my hip before cupping my ass as he drew my hips to his. I could already feel his erection growing, pressing into my belly. My knees grew weak, warmth spreading between my thighs.

"But there are so many other details we still have to figure out."

"We have time for all that," he whispered, bringing his lips to my ear, nibbling on my lobe before trailing his tongue down my neck, teasing my skin. His touch sent shivers down my spine, and I let him lead me to his bed.

After all, he was right.

For once, we had all the time in the world.

Epilogue

Valentina

"Need a little help there, darlin'?" Duke asked as he walked into our master bathroom and found me struggling to get my necklace clasped around my neck.

"That would be great, thanks, babe." I handed him the delicate gold chain, which he easily maneuvered around my neck, fastening the little clasp with a small click of his tongue.

"*Muy bonita*," he said, sliding his hands over my shoulders and down my hips, admiring the reflection of my form-fitting maroon dress in the mirror. He pulled my tumbling curls to one side and placed his lips softly on my neck, sending happy shivers down my spine.

I reached back and ran my fingers through his tousled hair, letting my nails dig a little into his scalp, and he responded by nipping my delicate skin, not so hard that it hurt, but just enough to cause a tingle between my legs.

"If you keep that up, we're going to be late to your party," I purred, arching my back and pushing my behind against his groin. He groaned into my neck, taking a deep breath in as his hands roamed freely over my body.

"You tempt me." His voice was muffled as he spoke into my skin, giving me one last kiss before pulling away. Already my body missed his touch, but I was right. You'd think that a full year and a half together would have tamped out some of the fire between us, but if anything, it had only made it burn brighter and way more intense. Both of our sex drives were through the roof, and we were starting to get a reputation for being late to things, something we were secretly proud of. But still, tonight was different. The event we were attending was too important to be late to.

I checked myself in the mirror, adjusting the neckline of my dress and rearranging my hair around my shoulders before following Duke to the car. He opened the passenger side door for me, giving my rear a little pat as I climbed in. It was the kind of small thing that I used to roll my eyes at, but after a year and a half together, it was sweet that he still took the time for gestures like that—with a little bit of Duke playfulness thrown in there too.

"Nervous?" I asked, reaching across the center console and taking his hand in mine. He rubbed his thumb over my knuckles, turning to give me a sideways dimpled smile.

"With you by my side? Never."

He brought my fingers to his lips, pressing them against my knuckles. I smiled, a warm, contented feeling washing over me, followed quickly by regret that we had somewhere to be and couldn't pull over somewhere for a quickie. *Good Lord, I'm hornier now than I was in high school.*

We pulled up into the parking lot of the distillery, which was slowly filling up with cars. Vintage string lights had been hung up all throughout the back patio of the tasting room, casting a warm, inviting glow over the space. Inside, the tables were all set with gold silverware and place settings, with huge centerpieces full of wildflowers in the middle.

"Charlotte really outdid herself this time," I murmured as we walked through the door. Duke nodded, taking it all in, a small, appreciative smile spreading across his face.

"City slicker knows how to throw a party, that's for sure."

"You know Charlotte and I are both from cities, right?"

"LA and New York are pretty different cities, darlin'."

"All I'm saying is it might be time to find a different thing to tease her about. Besides, you know she's a little more sensitive than usual these days."

Duke shrugged just as Charlotte and Luke arrived behind us, the fabric of Charlotte's pale blue shimmering dress stretching over her swollen belly. She squealed when she saw us and quickly waddled over to us, the excited noise quickly followed by immediate tears welling up in the corners of her eyes.

"Oh, Char, this place almost looks as beautiful as you do," I said, wrapping my arms around her. Even after seven months, I still wasn't used to the new distance between us when we hugged. Which was often. Pregnancy had made Charlotte more emotional than ever. And as crazy as it was that my best friend in the whole world was literally brewing a new human inside her, I was more grateful than ever to be living in Shady Grove so I could be with her and experience the freaking miracle of it all with her every step of the way.

"Val, you seriously can't say things like that!" she cried, grabbing a napkin from a nearby table and dabbing at her eyes with it. "At least let me make it through cocktail hour before I lose all my mascara."

I rubbed her back as we joined the boys, who were pouring themselves each a glass of whiskey at the bar.

"Can I get one of those?" I nodded to Duke's glass, and he responded by handing it to me, wordlessly pouring himself another. I smiled and kissed his cheek in thanks.

"Ugh, I'm so proud of you two," Charlotte gushed, placing a hand on Luke and Duke's shoulders. "Winning the Best in Texas award for Excellence in Whiskey within the first couple years of statewide distribution? That's unheard of. The Wilder men are a force to be reckoned with, that's for sure."

"Thank you, duchess," Luke said, leaning over and planting a kiss on her lips.

Duke turned to me and raised an eyebrow.

"For the record, I'm proud of you guys too," I said. "Char's pregnancy glow is hard to top, though."

We all laughed, and the men ushered us to our table to drop our purses before the rest of the crowd showed up.

We'd gotten the call that Wilder Whiskey was being honored this award season about a month ago. If opening the tasting room and expanding distribution statewide was Duke's dream come true, this award was his wet dream. We decided that we had to celebrate in the biggest way we could think of, and given Charlotte's years of experience throwing impressive dinner parties and events in New York, we thought a full-on red carpet style night of celebration would be fitting. We invited the whole town and pulled out all the stops, which included a catered dinner, a full band from a few towns over, and the unveiling of a new signature champagne and bourbon cocktail, Bourbon and Bubbles.

As people began milling in, the whole town dressed to the nines, Luke and Duke stood near the entrance of the distillery, greeting everyone as they arrived. I loved how hands-on they still were, despite how quickly things were taking off. Watching Duke in action always made me swell up with pride, though I was hesitant to gush over him as easily as Charlotte did for Luke. I'd learned over the course of our relationship that that kind of attention had the tendency to only go to his head, whereas a serious conversation at the end of the day could serve as a meaningful reminder that I saw how hard he was working and appreciated it. But then again, what did I know? It still felt like I was learning something new every day in this relationship, and I loved every twist and turn.

"Oh my God, Val, you're an absolute vision in that dress." I turned to find Molly standing behind me, dressed in a floor-length gauzy rose-colored number that made her look like a fairy princess. Her hair was curled and pinned back loosely around her temples, which only made her trademark Wilder green eyes pop even more.

"Aw, thank you, Mols, you're always way too sweet to me."

"Are you kidding? That plunging neckline, the midi-length, the way it hugs your curves, that color against your skin? I mean, you always look good, but this is a whole other level."

I smiled and shook my head. Molly and I had gotten close since I decided to move to Shady Grove for good, and a few months back she even started helping me with some of the remote work I was doing for the firm. She might not know anything about law, but damn, that Molly Wilder could keep track of a schedule and get ahold of a flaky client.

"Well, you don't look so bad yourself, Mols. I'm loving the way this color complements your eyes."

A blush crept over Molly's cheeks, just in time for Charlotte to return from the bathroom to join us at our table near the front of the room, close to the makeshift stage.

"Oh my god, Charlotte! Look at your belly! I feel like it's grown at least another inch since I last saw you."

"Don't I know it. This baby is going to be a bitch to squeeze out."

"Char!"

"What? I've talked to enough women with infants to know what's in store for me. But that doesn't mean I love my little honeybun any less," she cooed, placing her hands on her belly and smiling down at it.

"Well, we can't wait to meet him," I added.

"It's a him? I thought you guys decided you wanted to be surprised!"

"We did," Charlotte said, narrowing her eyes at me. "Val here just has an active imagination."

"I just have a feeling," I shrugged, tossing back the last of my drink.

Molly looked between us, her face an equal mix of happy and sad.

"You two are so lucky," she sighed, taking her glass in her hand and swirling the amber liquid. "If I don't find someone soon in this one-horse town, I'll be doomed to die alone."

"Oh, Molly, that's not true," Charlotte insisted, furrowing her brow and rubbing Molly's back. Molly forced a weak smile and sighed, to which I clucked my tongue.

"Molly, listen. I'm about to tell you what my mother always told me. These kinds of things always happen when you least expect it. The most important thing you can do is work on loving yourself and becoming the person you want to be. Everything else will happen when it's supposed to."

"Easy for you to say," she grumbled, her eyes darting to the front of the room, where Luke and Duke were schmoozing with some of the older men of the town.

"Do you think either of us were looking for love when we came to Shady Grove?" Charlotte asked, cocking her head to the side.

"Mols, you know better than anyone how unexpected things between your brother and me were," I added. "This couldn't be further from how I thought my life would turn out. And don't get me wrong, it hasn't always been easy. There have been some real rough patches here and there, a lot of changes to adjust to. But through it all, there's been a part of me that just knew Duke was who I wanted to be with. Even if that meant I couldn't make the two-hour drive to get a good taco as often as I wanted."

Molly snorted at my joke, and I smiled, placing my hand over hers on the table.

"You'll find someone, Molly. I know it."

"Yeah well, if you two are any example, it sounds like I need to get out of Shady Grove to find him."

Charlotte and I shared a look. That was exactly something we'd discussed on more than one occasion, the idea that spending time somewhere new could be good for Molly.

"It might not hurt," Charlotte said, "but if you're going to do that, do it soon and get back here before I have this baby because Lord knows we're going to need help with childcare."

We all laughed, just as Luke and Duke joined us at the table, each raising an inquisitive brow.

"What are you ladies giggling about?" Duke asked, taking his seat next to me.

"Whatever it is, it can't be good," Luke added, sliding an arm across Charlotte's shoulders.

"Nothing," Molly said, shooting us a look that told us to zip it. She was funny like that sometimes, an open book one second and clamming up the next. My heart ached thinking that watching her brothers find love made her feel lonely. But for as hopeless as Molly felt about her love life sometimes, there was no doubt in my mind she'd find someone soon.

Once everyone took their seats, Luke gave a short speech thanking everyone for coming and explaining what a huge honor it was to be recognized in that way. In typical Luke fashion, he kept it brief, sincere, and to the point, toasting his brother and all the hard work they'd put in over the past almost twelve years.

When Luke was done, the wait staff kicked off the meal with a first course of watermelon, balsamic, and feta salads, a far cry from the greasy, butter-soaked sides this town was used to. They had Charlotte and me to thank for that. Luke and Duke let us take full control of the menu. All they asked is that we made sure there was a decent cut of red meat in the main course.

The band played some lively music while we ate, nothing too crazy, but definitely not the kind of smooth jazz you'd expect at a Manhattan dinner party. After all, we were still in

Shady Grove. A representative from the Best in Texas voting board joined us for the evening and sat at our table. He was a lot cooler and younger than I was expecting, and judging by his suspenders and bow-tie, my guess was he was one of those hipster types.

Near the end of the first course, one of the wait staff arrived at Duke's side and whispered something in his ear. He furrowed his brow at whatever the man said, nodding solemnly. Once he left, Duke turned and placed his hand on my lower back, leaning over to whisper in my ear.

"There's something wrong in the brew room. They need me to go check it out."

Before I could answer, he was out of his seat and halfway to the door, pushing his hand roughly through his hair like he did when he was stressed. I stared after him, annoyed that something was taking him away from his own celebration event. He was always hard on himself, and something going wrong in the brew room on such an important night didn't bode well for his overall well-being.

I turned back to the table to find Charlotte and Luke watching me, worried looks on their faces.

"Everything okay?" Luke asked, looking ready to jump up and join his brother at any moment.

"Yeah, don't worry about it. Something in the brew room, I guess."

Luke nodded, but he didn't look satisfied. Charlotte and Molly shared a strange look, and I could have sworn Molly was almost smirking, but I just shook it off. Something weird was going on, but I didn't care what it was. I just wanted Duke to come back and let himself enjoy his night.

By the time the main course was being cleared away for dessert, Duke still hadn't returned, and I was really starting to worry about him. I tried my best to act normal in front of the Best of Texas rep, but inside, I was freaking out. *What if one of the tanks exploded? What if one of the tanks fell on him and he's suffocating underneath it? Why is no one else freaking out right now?*

I watched Charlotte chat easily with Luke and Molly, frustration bubbling up within me. They all seemed so calm, so unbothered by my boyfriend's disappearance, and I'd had just about enough of it. Craning my neck, I scanned the room for the twentieth time, searching for any sign of Duke, or any sign of distress among the wait staff. But there was nothing. Everyone seemed cool and collected as cucumbers, and it was annoying the shit out of me.

"This is ridiculous," I muttered, setting my napkin on the table and scooting my chair back. This got Charlotte's attention, and she looked at me with wide, worried eyes.

"Where are you going?"

"To find Duke. He's been gone for like half an hour now. I think something's really wrong."

"No, you'll ruin it!" Molly exclaimed, quickly clapping a hand over her mouth as soon as the words left her lips.

"Molly!" Charlotte hissed.

"What do you—"

But before I could finish my sentence, Duke magically reappeared through the front door with two women, one on each arm. I had to blink a few times to make sure my eyes weren't playing tricks on me. Tears stung my eyes as I took in the women, the one on his left with curly dark hair like mine and a kind face, the one on his right with her gray hair swept back into a neat bun at the base of her neck.

They weren't just any women. It was my mom and grandma, here in Shady Grove for the first time since I decided to stay here.

"Mama! Abuela!"

The whole room watched as I stood and rushed to them, throwing my arms around both their necks at the same time. Tears fell freely down my cheeks and onto their brightly patterned dresses, but I didn't care. They were here, in the flesh, and I could hold them, touch them. They both cried too, smoothing my curls and gently shushing me, just like they used to do when I was little.

It's not like I hadn't seen them since the move. I'd gone back to LA a couple times over the past eighteen months, and we talked on the phone as often as we could, but no matter how often we talked, I missed them, always. So being surprised with them in that moment was one of the most special things that had happened to me in a long time.

And that was just the beginning.

When I finally released Mom and Abuela, I kissed Duke hard, throwing my arms around his neck and peppering him with thank yous. He smiled, laughing and kissing me back, before setting me firmly back on the ground.

"Wait here," he said.

He then walked to the stage, where the lead singer of the band gave him the mic with a knowing smile. Butterflies filled my stomach as I watched Duke grab the mic and take a deep breath. For the first time in a long time, he looked nervous. And that could only mean one thing.

"Ladies and gentleman, I'm sorry to interrupt your evening, but I have something important to say."

The room quieted, and everyone turned their attention to Duke. I took my mother's hand in one hand and my abuela's in the other, bracing myself for one hell of an emotional rollercoaster.

"Wilder Whiskey has always been about family. As many of you know, our father left us this place in a pretty bad state. It was hard, but my brother and I turned it all around with a lot of hard work in a few years' time, and we couldn't have done it without the support of our sister and of the entire community. Then, just when I thought we were on top of the world, a little legal trouble came our way, threatening everything we worked so hard for. At the time, it was devastating, but little did I know, that legal trouble would bring a woman into my life who would change everything, including what I wanted my family to look like."

Aww's erupted around the room, and many people turned to look at me, but I barely even noticed them. My eyes were glued on Duke, the love of my life, standing in front of literally everyone we knew, talking about me.

"Valentina, I know you never envisioned yourself living in a small town. You've sacrificed so much to be with me, to give this thing a real shot, and for that alone, I'll be forever grateful. I love you, darlin', and you've made me happier than I thought was ever possible. That being said, I was hoping I could ask you one more thing."

My stomach dropped. *Oh my God, it's happening. It's really fucking happening.*

"Will you marry me?"

Tears streamed down my face, and it felt like my heart was exploding out of my chest. I realized I was squeezing the life out of Mom and Abuela's hands, so I let them go, turning to look at them with wide, searching eyes.

They smiled at me, wiping the tears from my cheeks with their soft thumbs.

"I think he's waiting for you, *mija*," my mom said, chuckling softly.

"*Lo amamos,*" my abuela said, cupping my face with her hand and turning my head to look at Duke.

I practically floated to his side on stage, only vaguely aware of the number of teary eyes watching us. When I stood in front of him, Duke got down on one knee, and the whole room sighed and gasped at the sight. He pulled a little black velvet box out of his suit pocket, and inside were my mother and grandmother's wedding bands, fused on either side of the most perfect rock I'd ever seen.

"What do you say, darlin'?"

I laughed, a fresh new batch of tears brimming in my eyes as I looked down at that dimpled smile, those glittering green eyes I loved waking up to. It was simple. The simplest decision I'd ever made in my life.

"Yes. I say yes."

* * * *

Also from 1001 Dark Nights and Kendall Ryan, discover The Bed Mate.

Sign up for the 1001 Dark Nights Newsletter
and be entered to win a Tiffany Key necklace.

There's a contest every month!

Go to www.1001DarkNights.com to subscribe.

As a bonus, all subscribers will receive a free copy of
Discovery Bundle Three
Featuring stories by
Sidney Bristol, Darcy Burke, T. Gephart
Stacey Kennedy, Adriana Locke
JB Salsbury, and Erika Wilde

Discover 1001 Dark Nights Collection Five

Go to www.1001DarkNights.com for more information.

BLAZE ERUPTING by Rebecca Zanetti
Scorpius Syndrome/A Brigade Novella

ROUGH RIDE by Kristen Ashley
A Chaos Novella

HAWKYN by Larissa Ione
A Demonica Underworld Novella

RIDE DIRTY by Laura Kaye
A Raven Riders Novella

ROME'S CHANCE by Joanna Wylde
A Reapers MC Novella

THE MARRIAGE ARRANGEMENT by Jennifer Probst
A Marriage to a Billionaire Novella

SURRENDER by Elisabeth Naughton
A House of Sin Novella

INKED NIGHT by Carrie Ann Ryan
A Montgomery Ink Novella

ENVY by Rachel Van Dyken
An Eagle Elite Novella

PROTECTED by Lexi Blake
A Masters and Mercenaries Novella

THE PRINCE by Jennifer L. Armentrout
A Wicked Novella

PLEASE ME by J. Kenner
A Stark Ever After Novella

WOUND TIGHT by Lorelei James
A Rough Riders/Blacktop Cowboys Novella®

STRONG by Kylie Scott
A Stage Dive Novella

DRAGON NIGHT by Donna Grant
A Dark Kings Novella

TEMPTING BROOKE by Kristen Proby
A Big Sky Novella

HAUNTED BE THE HOLIDAYS by Heather Graham
A Krewe of Hunters Novella

CONTROL by K. Bromberg
An Everyday Heroes Novella

HUNKY HEARTBREAKER by Kendall Ryan
A Whiskey Kisses Novella

THE DARKEST CAPTIVE by Gena Showalter
A Lords of the Underworld Novella

Discover 1001 Dark Nights Collection One

Go to www.1001DarkNights.com for more information.

Discover 1001 Dark Nights Collection Two

Go to www.1001DarkNights.com for more information.

WICKED WOLF by Carrie Ann Ryan
WHEN IRISH EYES ARE HAUNTING by Heather Graham
EASY WITH YOU by Kristen Proby
MASTER OF FREEDOM by Cherise Sinclair
CARESS OF PLEASURE by Julie Kenner
ADORED by Lexi Blake
HADES by Larissa Ione
RAVAGED by Elisabeth Naughton
DREAM OF YOU by Jennifer L. Armentrout
STRIPPED DOWN by Lorelei James
RAGE/KILLIAN by Alexandra Ivy/Laura Wright
DRAGON KING by Donna Grant
PURE WICKED by Shayla Black
HARD AS STEEL by Laura Kaye
STROKE OF MIDNIGHT by Lara Adrian
ALL HALLOWS EVE by Heather Graham
KISS THE FLAME by Christopher Rice
DARING HER LOVE by Melissa Foster
TEASED by Rebecca Zanetti
THE PROMISE OF SURRENDER by Liliana Hart

Also from 1001 Dark Nights

THE SURRENDER GATE By Christopher Rice
SERVICING THE TARGET By Cherise Sinclair

Discover 1001 Dark Nights Collection Three

Go to www.1001DarkNights.com for more information.

HIDDEN INK by Carrie Ann Ryan
BLOOD ON THE BAYOU by Heather Graham
SEARCHING FOR MINE by Jennifer Probst
DANCE OF DESIRE by Christopher Rice
ROUGH RHYTHM by Tessa Bailey
DEVOTED by Lexi Blake
Z by Larissa Ione
FALLING UNDER YOU by Laurelin Paige
EASY FOR KEEPS by Kristen Proby
UNCHAINED by Elisabeth Naughton
HARD TO SERVE by Laura Kaye
DRAGON FEVER by Donna Grant
KAYDEN/SIMON by Alexandra Ivy/Laura Wright
STRUNG UP by Lorelei James
MIDNIGHT UNTAMED by Lara Adrian
TRICKED by Rebecca Zanetti
DIRTY WICKED by Shayla Black
THE ONLY ONE by Lauren Blakely
SWEET SURRENDER by Liliana Hart

Discover 1001 Dark Nights Collection Four

Go to www.1001DarkNights.com for more information.

About Kendall Ryan

A *New York Times*, *Wall Street Journal*, and *USA TODAY* bestselling author of more than two dozen titles, Kendall Ryan has sold over two million books, and her books have been translated into several languages in countries around the world. Her books have also appeared on the *New York Times* and *USA TODAY* bestseller list more than three dozen times. Kendall has been featured in publications such as *USA TODAY*, *Newsweek*, and *In Touch Magazine*. She lives in Texas with her husband and two sons.

Website: www.kendallryanbooks.com
Facebook: Kendall Ryan Books
Twitter: @kendallryan1
Instagram: *www.instagram.com/kendallryan1*
Newsletter: www.kendallryanbooks.com/newsletter/

Get an alert when I release a book or put a title on sale. Sign up here: www.bookbub.com/authors/kendall-ryan

Sexy Stranger
By Kendall Ryan

From *New York Times* Bestselling author Kendall Ryan comes a sexy and sizzling, enemies-to-lovers romp with bite.

He's rude. Arrogant. And too hot to handle.

And she's stranded with him for an entire week.

He knows the sexy stranger doesn't belong in his small town, but he's determined to keep her there. The second she opens her smart mouth, he wants to swap a whole lot more than insults with her. She's got a secret. But he's got his own agenda.

Buckle up.

Discover More Kendall Ryan

The Bed Mate
By Kendall Ryan

I might be a typical guy, but these last few years, my love life's been anything but. From crazy ex-girlfriends to one-night stands who are stage-five clingers, my relationships go bad faster than the milk in your fridge. The only constant has been my best friend Maggie.

Fresh off a bad breakup of her own, I invite Maggie to my guys' skiing weekend knowing she needs an escape from reality. But then something funny starts to happen. I start noticing things about her that I never noticed before.

She's beautiful and doesn't know it, she's funny without even trying, and now she's suddenly single for the first time in forever.

Sharing a hotel room with her proves to be the tipping point in our very platonic friendship. Suddenly I want to put my hands, my mouth, and my...other parts...all over her gorgeous body. I want to claim her, make sure no man touches her ever again.

But am I ready to screw up the best relationship I've ever had for a shot at something more?

On behalf of 1001 Dark Nights,

Liz Berry and M.J. Rose would like to thank ~

Steve Berry
Doug Scofield
Kim Guidroz
Jillian Stein
InkSlinger PR
Dan Slater
Asha Hossain
Chris Graham
Fedora Chen
Kasi Alexander
Jessica Johns
Dylan Stockton
Richard Blake
and Simon Lipskar

Made in the USA
Columbia, SC
25 November 2018